D0273032

This Walker book belongs to:

_____

_____

WAKEFIELD LIBRARIES

30000010318361

Published 2014 by Walker Books Ltd
87 Vauxhall Walk, London SE11 5HJ

10 9 8 7 6 5 4 3 2 1

Text © 2012 Sally Sutton
Illustrations © 2012 Robyn Belton

The right of Sally Sutton and Robyn Belton to be identified as author
and illustrator respectively of this work has been asserted by them
in accordance with the Copyright, Designs and Patents Act 1988

This book has been typeset in Baskerville and Caslon Antique

Printed in China

All rights reserved. No part of this book may be reproduced, transmitted
or stored in an information retrieval system in any form or by any means,
graphic, electronic or mechanical, including photocopying, taping and
recording, without prior written permission from the publisher.

British Library Cataloguing in Publication Data:
a catalogue record for this book is available from the British Library

ISBN 978-1-4063-5187-3

www.walker.co.uk

For Reuben and James – S. S.
For Anton – R. B.

With thanks to
the Thornbury Vintage Tractor
Museum, the Geraldine Vintage Car
Machinery Museum and Ted. R. B.

WAKEFIELD LIBRARIES & INFO. SERVICES	
30000010318361	
Bertrams	15/07/2014
ANL	£6.99

Farmer John's Tractor

by **SALLY SUTTON** *Illustrated by* **ROBYN BELTON**

WALKER BOOKS
AND SUBSIDIARIES

LONDON • BOSTON • SYDNEY • AUCKLAND

Farmer John's tractor lies locked in the shed,
Rusty yet trusty and orangey-red.

That winter the rain comes. It rains and it rains.

It fills up the river and blocks up the drains.

The riverbanks break. It's a flood! Water swirls.

It rushes and gushes. It spurts and it twirls.

From down by the river, there comes a great shout:

"Please help! Our car's stranded! We cannot get out!"

But Farmer John's tractor lies locked in the shed,
Rusty yet trusty and orangey-red.

From far down the roadway, a jeep's coming near.

It speeds through the water. The girls give a cheer.

But how could they guess what these deep waters hide?

A rock! With a splash, the jeep rolls on its side!

Along comes a tow truck, as strong as can be.

"Hold fast," calls the driver, "I'll soon set you free!"

But look how its wheels spin around in the muck.

It sinks ever deeper – this tow truck is stuck!

The girls clamber onto the roof of the car.

The water's still rising. How frightened they are!

And Farmer John's tractor lies locked in the shed,
Rusty yet trusty and orangey-red.

A fire engine's coming! It's noisy and fast.

Its siren is wailing. Its horn gives a blast.

It speeds round the hillside, but right on the dip

It slams to a halt – on the road is a slip!

The fire engine's useless. It has to reverse.

The crew's looking worried; the flood's getting worse.

Still Farmer John's tractor lies locked in the shed,
Rusty yet trusty and orangey-red.

The girls start to shake and to quake and to sob.

Oh, surely there's someone who's up to the job?

What's this? Farmer John's by the shed with a key!

He unlocks the padlock. The tractor is free!

It grunts, then it splutters and starts with a roar,

And Farmer John's tractor chugs out of the door!

The girls see him coming, but how can they trust

This clanking old tractor, all covered in rust?

At last, Farmer John pulls up right by their side.

"Hop on! Squeeze together! Let's go for a ride!"

Then Mum and Dad cheer, and the girls shout, "Hooray!

Thanks, Farmer John's tractor! You've rescued the day!"

They're safe and they're happy,

And free from all harm,

So Farmer John's tractor chugs back to the farm …

Never again to be locked in the shed,
Rusty yet trusty and orangey-red.

SALLY SUTTON is the author of the award-winning *Roadworks* and *Demolition*, and is also a playwright. She lives in Auckland, New Zealand, with her husband and two daughters.

ROBYN BELTON is one of New Zealand's best-known and most celebrated children's-book illustrators and the winner of many awards, including the prestigious Margaret Mahy Medal. In addition to her work as a professional illustrator, she has taught and run workshops for both children and adults and has had her work exhibited all over the world.

LOOK OUT FOR:

978-1-4063-2537-9

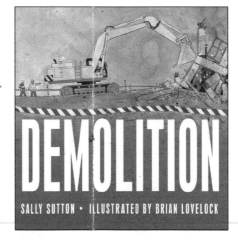

978-1-4063-3936-9

Available from all good booksellers

www.walker.co.uk